Scrib.~~b.b.~~bles

from the Middling Cat

INTERRELATED ENTRIES

A

SEQUEL TO

HAEE AND THE

OTHER

MIDDLINGS

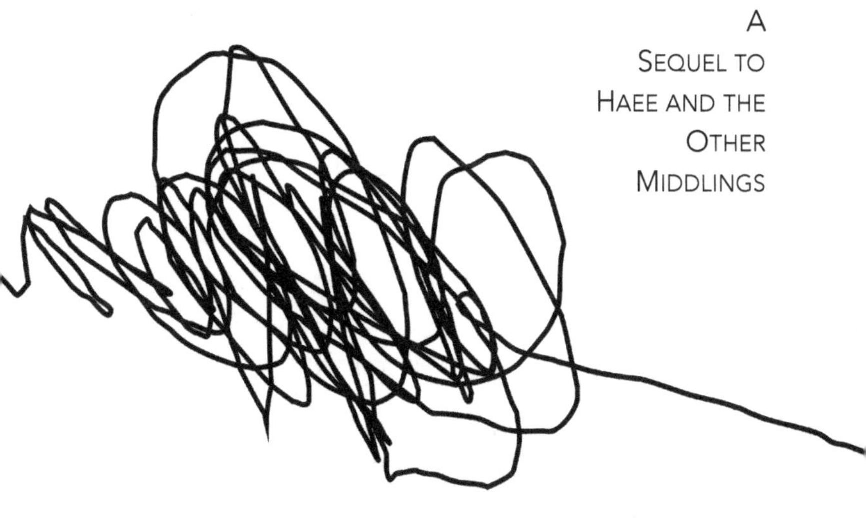

Scrib.~~b.b.~~bles

from the Middling Cat

INTERRELATED ENTRIES

R.S. Vern

MIDDLING

INDUSTRIES

By R.S. Vern

Illustrated Book Series

Haee and the Other Middlings
Part One/ Haee The Cat with a Crooked Tail
Part Two/ The Unconventional Life of Haee
Part Three/ Haee's Quest for the Greater Prairie

Prose and Poems

Scribbles from the Middling Cat

Should you wish to contact the Publisher, please send your enquiries to rights@middlingindustries.com.

Scribbles from the Middling Cat
Digital book
ISBN 978-9-8118-6863-4
Paperback
ISBN 978-9-8118-6862-7
Hardcover
ISBN 978-9-8118-7111-5

Published by Middling Industries
www.middlingindustries.com

Publisher's Note

This is fiction. For all ages.

Scribbles is a collection of random notes written by cat Haee, a middling cat. We encourage you to read only when you are alone.

If you find any similarities of yourself in cat Haee, it is purely out of coincidence or a result of the author's daydreams.

Or you could just be one serious fellow middling.

Read more about cat Haee and the other intriguing characters from award winning illustrated book series "Haee and the Other Middlings".

*Dear **Reader**,*

Fiction or not, I am a middling cat taken from trilogy book series "Haee and the Other Middlings" by R.S. Vern. I spend most of my time alone and day-dreaming. That gives me plenty of time to contemplate on life.

I have a curious eye in Humanities. My favourite colour is white. "The Outsider" by Albert Camus is one of the books I turn to whenever insomnia gets me. I spend a lot of time wondering about what happens when I am alone and dying.

Musing,
Haee

Definition

Middlings commonly have a comfortable standard of living, considerable economic security, moderate work + life autonomy and often rely on their own expertise to sustain themselves.

They place great emphasis on independence, value innovation, respect the non-conformist and have great concerns for the environment. They appear established and well-rounded but, often have insecurities locked within.

Middlings live among others but essentially feel apart from it all.

They often ask themselves this: "Are we just not as happy as those who are much better off in this world?"

PART I

Middlings have no time to think

Friday, January 6, evening

I have come to realise middlings do work very hard. Possibly 14 hours a day.

To live.

We have no time to think.

STIFLING STREETS I CANNOT GET OUT OF

Friday, February 10, afternoon

The heat in the streets is stifling. The stuffiness, jostling crowds, traffic noise, polluted air, undiluted dust and, the peculiar stench of summer in the city so familiar to those who are living in it and, cannot get away from it. All combined to aggravate my already agitated nerves.

MUTTER TO SELF

Friday, February 10, evening

I mutter to myself.
Once. Twice. Repeat.
Like tape gone bad.

The weather is getting humid. The traffic is getting bad. The weather is getting humid. The traffic is getting bad.

Does it ever get better?

It is Friday night. This manner of self-muttering has grown habitual for me. Even in thoughts.

That Accidental Couple

Tuesday, February 14, morning

Did you say something?
No.
How's the weather?
...
Had your dose?
No.
What's today's date?
14 Feb.
Wanna celebrate?
...

A VISIT TO THE FILTHY PUBLIC HOUSE

Wednesday, February 15, afternoon

I am not used to the crowds. I tend to avoid most social contacts. But today, I feel drawn to people. I want to feel the heat, the thirst for some contact, be among them. I long to breathe and so, in spite of the usual fear, I take pleasure a visit to the filthy public house filled with loud music, booze, and cigarettes.

ONE HUNDRED AND FORTY FOUR STEPS

Thursday, February 16, morning

I know exactly how many steps it takes from the flat to the bin downstairs – one hundred and forty four. Today, there are an additional five steps, just to avoid the mess around the corner.

MIDDLINGS' STRESS. DO YOU EVER FEEL IT?

Friday, February 17, evening

1) Stress from being over worked + long hours of commutes + lack of sleep
2) Depression and anxiety at being skipped over for a promotion
3) Losing one's job
4) Being denied a bonus expected as a reward for hard work
5) Loss of status and respect that comes with being denied a promotion or being laid off

Get a dog

Monday, February 20, morning

Everything is a test of perseverance, tolerance, and love - of how much they would endure in order to stay together. They thought drinking could be the problem. They stayed sober. No more hangovers, lots of energy, everything had never looked so clear. They thought they had conquered the problem.

I'm not the one with the problem, he says. You're the one with the problem.

I decide to go take a walk in the park and think about if it's any worth getting a dog instead.

No speck of dust

Tuesday, February 21, afternoon

Old furniture belongs in this old flat.
One lonely crusty chair. A stained mirror
sits by the side table. A telephone
that never rings.

I sit in front of the 25 inch box, sip
plain water. Everything has its time
and place. No speck of dust.
Just quiet.

Art installation

Wednesday, February 22, evening

I was in a peculiar mood. Of course, even before dinner was over, I managed to ask myself the habitual question: "Why haven't I left?"

From time to time, I looked at my family but they completely ignored me. In the end, I got angry and decided to be offensive. I left them this piece of art installation.

I AM A UNIT OF LABOR, A CONSUMER AND A TAXPAYER. I AM A MIDDLING.

Thursday, February 23, afternoon

Big business looks at me either as a unit of labor or a consumer. Big media sees me as a consumer or a unit of audience measurement. And if I am in the middle class, I am just a taxpayer to the government.

We need decent affordable retirement villages.

Friday, February 24, morning

I know I am just a cat. I shouldn't be thinking about this. But the reality is, I am single, alone, and growing old. I don't wish to depend on anyone as I age (not that I have any). I'll like to live in some retirement villages with decent, dignified facilities at affordable costs. But the city is getting crowded and expensive. Mars?

MMM - Morose Moron Me

Monday, February 27, morning

I sometimes think of myself as a fly, like a gimp. This long crooked tail of mine makes me sensitive, touchy, quick to take offence. How annoying!

But do you know there are more than 10 ways to kill a fly? I'll share 2 here.

1 Do it early in the day. Flies are cold-blooded. The reactions of insects depend on the temperature in the air. They tend to be a bit dopey either in the early mornings or evenings. But in the heat of the day, they will be very quick.

2 Use chopsticks like in the movie "Karate Kid". Mr Miyagi's advice - "Man who catches fly with chopsticks accomplishes anything".

The problem with entitlement

Tuesday, February 28, evening

I don't have a problem with entitlement. The problem is I'm not getting what I want. Owning a house is not just for the rich. It's also for the middlings who want to be in debt (like forever).

Hot sweaty crowded and alone

Friday, March 2, evening

I stay up endless nights, murmur
to anybody, hoping to find some
conversation in this hot sweaty crowded
city.

I implore to all stars, dead and alive. Sing
with me, be my orchestra. Play my strings,
so I play yours.

This uncomfortable acid silence, eroding
my self-consciousness, lay me bare
in this hot sweaty crowded city.

I crouch in my old corner, seeking
something I can never seem to find, but
my own garden of weeds.

I am left eyes wide shut.
"Is anybody there?"

I DON'T LIKE SUNDAYS

Sunday, March 4, afternoon

I don't like Sundays. I sleep till eleven. Stay in bed. Smoke a few cigarettes till noon. I rummage through the junk, eat some stuff out from the bin. No leftover beer because Tom usually finishes them on Saturday nights. And I spend the rest of the day in front of the 25 inch box. It's quiet. I look forward to Mondays. I'll let you know why.

MONDAY MORNING POKER

Monday, March 5, morning

I like Monday mornings. The pavements are a little grimy after the weekends but everyone out and about, all walk in a hurry. Their strides are purposeful. Hurrying to catch a tram, a bus, or subway. They have a lot on their minds. You can tell from their seriously robotic faces. If everyone plays poker with this kind of face, it could take a while to eventually thin out the competition.

Recession: A Vicious Cycle or a Virtuous One?

Monday, March 12, evening

There is a general shrinking demand and consumption due to wage freezes and layoffs.

People are buying more used cars rather than new cars.

Young people are living with parents rather than moving out due to high housing costs.

I wonder if this recession is a vicious cycle or a virtuous one.

Control Alt Delete

Wednesday, March 14, afternoon

The room feels stuffy. The light flickers dimly. The wind howls outside. Some mouse scratches somewhere in a corner. The whole room smells of stale cigarettes and some kind of leather. I lay in a state of half-dream, with ideas chasing one another in my mind. I wish to find some object which my thoughts can fix themselves on. My thoughts. In night they build. In day they dismantle. When will they ever learn to behave? Control - alt - delete.

Breaking off and Breaking up

Monday, March 19, morning

sulphate of iron, 324mg
magnesia, 648mg
peppermint water, 713mg
spirit of nutmeg, 1 tsp

To be taken twice a day

This preparation acts as a tonic and stimulant, and so partly replaces the accustomed liquor, and prevents that absolute mental and physical prostration that follows a sudden breaking off from the use of stimulating drinks.

Use at your own risk but seems to have been proven useful since 1874.

If you have a wandering mind, you probably have sharper brains.

Monday, March 26, morning

That's right. You read it right. Studies have shown people who appear to be constantly distracted have more "working memory", giving us the ability to hold a lot of information in our heads and manipulate it mentally.

I feel assured.

"Farewell middle class! My lottery dream might just come true!"

Thursday, March 29, evening

"I keep thinking someone might just turn up at my door someday and hand me a million bucks, but it most probably might never happen."

"I just want to pay off my debts, support charities and save money for my children's college expenses."

That's right. Fact number one: Nobody wants to die poor. Fact number two: Everyone deserves to dream.

An over-used couch

Wednesday, April 4, afternoon

Sometimes I think of myself as a coward and a slave.

A coward because I don't dare fight this system I am in.

A slave because I rather follow blindly.

Perhaps it's not for a lack of courage to break out, but I'm just quite comfortable in front of this 25 inch box. That's what programming does to me.

I've been programmed not to think.
Like an over-used couch.

COMMUNICATIONS REVOLUTION + INCREASED LONGEVITY = SOLO LIVING

Tuesday, April 10, morning

I begin to think that solo living is an inevitable outgrowth of mainstream liberal values, in particular, the communications revolution. From telephone to Facebook, it has helped dissolve the boundary between social life and isolation. Plus given the increased longevity with medications. We are on track to making loners of people who have not previously lived by themselves.

Latchkey Cat

Friday, April 27, evening

I return to a familiar house, empty
of its contents.
An empty coke can, sits
frigid on the table top.
Time appears unstructured, as I
sit in front of the broken 25 inch box.
There is no moving image, only
me looking back at me.

Empty chair is my therapy

Friday, May 4, afternoon

I sometimes carry on long drawn conversations with an imagined person sitting on this empty chair. It gets rather therapeutic to the point I begin to think this imagined person is real and this empty chair is forever reserved for her.

Hungry. Angry. Lonely. Tired. What an awful combination.

Friday, May 18, evening

Several hours pass. I remain near my window, gazing out into the city. The traffic is busy but to me, it is almost motionless. I feel this deafening silence, until my ear is suddenly arrested by the footsteps outside the door, the turning of the lock. Finally, somebody is back to return my sanity.

Overpowered by Sleep in a Crowd

Monday, May 21, morning

I wandered about town like a restless spirit, separated from all, and miserable in the separation. When it was noon, I felt overpowered by a deep sleep. I had laid awake the whole of last night, my ears no longer sensitive, and my eyes inflamed by misery, smoked out by this crowd. When I awoke from my deep slumber, I felt as if I belonged once more, to a race of human beings like you. I guessed I just needed sleep.

SALE

What soberness conceals, drunkenness reveals.

Tuesday, June 12, morning

Tom re-filled his glass of fermented grape juice, drank it off and sat still, deep in thoughts. His hair and clothes had wisps of hay in them. I looked at him. He returned with sad, vacant eyes. I began to think, better to be in a state of stupor than in a state of clarity.

Selling Jane

Friday, June 22, evening

"I haven't read a single book in the longest time. I have been on the road the whole time. I am no longer highbrow. I am down among the realities of modern life. And what are these realities of modern life? The chief one is an everlasting, frantic struggle to sell things. With most people, it takes the form of selling themselves - getting a job and keeping it."

I AM MY BELLY MADE UP OF A FEW USELESS ORGANS.

Monday, July 9, evening

Boredom is inseparable from poverty. When you are under-fed and have nothing to do, you can interest yourself in nothing. When you lie on your bed all day, nothing will rouse you except food. Now I am just a belly made up of a few useless organs.

I AM ENTANGLED IN A WEB OF LIES.

Wednesday, July 11, afternoon

I stop cleaning my fur. The cigarette seller asks me why I am no longer smoking. I have letters I have to answer but stamps are too expensive. And meals are the most difficult of it all. I loaf around Central Park at meal-times, seemingly watching the pigeons. Afterwards, I smuggle food home in my pockets. My food is butter and bread, biscuits, and sometimes, wine. I mutter incoherently, so nobody will know the truth.

Perhaps Perhaps Perhaps

Monday, July 16, morning

Being a slave to money is a dead end road, for money can never bring in lasting happiness and peace. Perhaps. So why would people work eighty hours a week or put up with abusive bosses if having more money didn't matter?

Everything like Nothing

Wednesday, July 18, afternoon

This condition to feel nothing. No rage, no jealousy, no envy, no happiness and certainly no love. This new generation known to icily control and be inhumanly practical. Basing all decisions on logic, profitability and efficiency.

THE WAITER WHO WAITS AT THE CORNER

Friday, July 27, evening

The waiter works 13 hours a day, 7 days a week. He constantly sees money, hopes to get some, to some extent he comes to identify himself with his employer. There is always a chance the waiter may become rich himself.

Why is middling Jane a worrier?

Thursday, August 2, afternoon

Jane has chronic hives. She is allergic to peanuts, wheat, soy, dust and all kinds of preservatives. She has this haunted look about her, constantly soaping her hands, hiding her face underneath that massive chunk of hair. I can tell she is a worrier. But with a great husband, a stable job, sufficient income, what does she have to worry about?

I THINK I HAVE A BRAIN TUMOUR AND CAN I BECOME A SUPER PIG?

Monday, August 6, afternoon

But then again, is it ever possible for a cat to have a brain tumour? This incessant pull on my whiskers is annoying a nerve linked to my brain. It's a self-induced pain and it's certainly not a death wish I have. But when pain brings about a springboard in life, I jump at the chance of becoming something else other than a cat.

ANOMIE I AM

Wednesday, August 15, morning

Popularised by French sociologist Émile Durkheim , anomie is defined as a mismatch. Anomie is produced in a society with too much rigidity and little individual discretion, resulting in a mismatch between individual circumstances and larger social norms. Thus, fatalistic suicide arises when a person is too rule-governed, when there is no freedom even in thoughts.

- Wikipedia understands

24/7 SUNSCREEN PROVIDES SHELTER, SHADE, AND SOLITUDE

Thursday, August 16, afternoon

This persistent dark cloud over my head is annoying me. It's a 24/7 sunscreen. It blocks out the blazing light, screens out almost everything light, shutting out most of my senses, alienating me from the heat.

Keep out the menace

Tuesday, August 21, night

They say every man or cat for that matter should have enough vices to keep him from being a menace to society.

A Second Life

Thursday, August 23, morning

I don't remember a lot of things. My PDA usually reminds me. I don't need to know what the weather is like outside or what the weather is going to be like in the next 10 days. I've got 10 websites that tell me so. I don't have to visit places to learn. Wikipedia tells me what I need to know and Google Earth shows me what I want to see. And if I somehow misplace this life, I can always have a Second Life.

HOPE OUTSOURCED

Thursday, August 30, evening

Would you like to send kitty for potty
training classes?
Sure.
But you can only see the results when kitty
reaches 7 years old.
Ok. How much?
$5,000 for 10 classes.

Go blank

Tuesday, September 4, morning

Do the following to un-tense yourself although the final step is quite an art.

- look far away
- keep relaxing
- stay away from noisy places
- value the ability to make your mind a blank

Vending machine

Wednesday, September 26, afternoon

If you've ever eaten from the vending machine, you would understand that the dining experience is quick, efficient and pragmatic. There is no internal narrative, no dining experience, no sensory intake.

BIG LIFE

Friday, September 28, morning

We confuse a car with a home. We take up a loan to finance our cars, just like we take up a mortgage loan on our homes. In some cases we spend more waking hours in them (especially when you are stuck in a traffic jam). Cars have become a source of pride, as are our homes, which might be the reason why whenever circumstances allow they tend to get bigger.

Connected monster

Monday, October 1, afternoon

This expectation of constant connectivity is driving me insane with insecurities. My text message to her fails to elicit an immediate response. Clearly, she is angry. Or totally sick of me. Or dead in a ditch. I panic and behave badly. I send more texts. I want to know why I am being ignored and I end up spamming her inbox - leaving multiple messages across many different media within minutes.

No to the Stranger in Her Inbox

Wednesday, October 3, evening

Jane, in front of the computer typing with rigour to some random stranger:

"I appreciate your need to sell your product, make a living, and keep the economy going. But annoying me is not the best way to go. Perhaps you can find some other way to make work more interesting, helpful or, in some way contribute to the human race?"

PAY FOR PRIORITY

Friday, October 5, evening

You pay to get served first in a bank or at
an airline check-in counter.
You pay to get a priority seat in college.
You pay to get onto a highway lane with
no traffic jam.
You pay to get into an amusement park
without the hassle of waiting in line.
Just how much have you paid to get in
front?

A FINE DAY TO TEND MY GARDEN

Monday, October 8, morning

My gardener quits on a fine day. Weeds assail my garden. My bleeding rose counts her days. The foundation is rotting, infested with black flies. I hear some occasional digging out out on the porch, just scratching on old wounds.

I need more time to tend to my garden but I want to do it only on a fine day. Hang on. I hear someone's digging out again.

BEHOLD, TRUTH

Tuesday, October 16, afternoon

I sit in the corner for a good one afternoon. My eyes tracking Jane at her desk. She types furiously, letting out an occasional curse. She sits back, reads and re-reads her words, crumples the papers and takes bad aims at the waste bin. I say, she needs to unleash her words and not hold back the truth. Just what is she holding back? Does she not think we can handle the truth?

When you are this alone

Tuesday, October 23, morning

I tell you that man in the square has no friends in the world. He comes out only at night, smokes a pipe, sits by the fountain, and talks to random strangers. When the crowd thins, he goes upstairs. And repeats this routine again the next day. You really don't want to know what he thinks about everyday.

Houses, housing

Tuesday, October 30, afternoon

Do we revolve around houses or do houses revolve around us?

THE OUTSIDER

WORK IS THE FIRST RATE MEDICINE FOR ANY ILLNESS

Monday, November 5, afternoon

That's what I've been told. And I have been dreaming of being ill for the last few weeks. Not dangerously ill. Not so bad that I have to be operated on. But bad enough to go to the hospital and lie in bed for the next three weeks without stirring. Just feed me that cheap clear soup. I have no thoughts for the moment. My limbs have refused to work. I can't even find my tail.

Have you seen me today?

Thursday, November 8, evening

The old man has forgotten how to talk and how to think. He seems obsessed with just one question.

"How many people have walked past me without seeing me?"

Being different

Wednesday, November 14, evening

I don't really like people telling me what to do. What's wrong being different?

JUST DO IT JUST DOESN'T DO IT ANYMORE

Monday, November 19, morning

Ever since Nike's Just Do It slogan, we've always tried to maintain that positive can-do attitude. But do you ever realise you're working so much that you sometimes don't know how to turn it off? You feel the increased pressure to do more and more within that 24 hour time frame but with less and less tools. How do you ever start to disconnect at night when the tweeps are still tweeting?

Adolescence Can Be a Waking Nightmare

Thursday, November 22, morning

This disorder remains one of the least understood, least diagnosed, and most disabling of all anxiety disorders. Most are imprisoned in senseless rituals that siphon off energy that could otherwise contribute to their socio-economic functioning or personal development. This disorder sometimes persists into adulthood.

That's why I appreciate the dystopian space. It should never have been speculated.

THE 7 YEAR MARRIAGE CONTRACT

Friday, November 23, afternoon

This odd and sacred number will suffice for getting to know each other, producing a couple of children, separating and then getting back together again. You may have a honeymoon for the first 2 years. The next 4 in contentment and oblivion, making babies in between. Then one of the parties may grow more and more attentive as the end draws closer. The indifferent or discontented may be won over by this behaviour. Soon, you forget the passage of time and before you realise it, the term is up. Middle class marriages!

NERVOUS AND HARDLY MERRY

Friday, December 14, afternoon

The year is loosening its hold. Actions are dripping to a slow-mo. The lights are up and I hear Christmas carols. The weather has turned a nasty cold and I'm hardly a merry cat. All I want for Christmas is to avoid having a nervous breakdown.

NOT THE END OF THE WORLD

Friday, December 21, midnight

Looks like the Mayans got it wrong and why is this so depressing. Not that I am suicidal, but there really isn't much to think about when you vegetate in front of the 600 cable channels all day.

Merry Christmas

Tuesday, December 25, morning

Merry Christmas, middlings and TG I do not have a nervous breakdown.

COUNT DOWN TO A HAPPY NEW YEAR

Monday, December 31, morning

The world has never possessed so much. The world has never applied its knowledge so little. Though living, we forget to look up, breathe, smell, and feel. It is the jest for the future that makes us hold our heads up. Not pride nor arrogance. But a curiosity for the unknown is a form of future intelligence that seems totally innovative and motivating. On the dawn of the new year, it is up to us alone to reconstruct a more ambitious world. A world that feels more at one with itself!

PART II

GETTING BUMPED IN THE BRAND NEW YEAR

Friday, January 4, morning

First week into a new year and I'm totally consumed by insecurities. What's going to happen this year since the world did not end in the last. When jobs are scarce and technology are rapidly changing the ways people work and live. It feels like an uphill climb for someone like me to want to get into the pace again after the holidays. I'm walking but I keep getting bumped.

"I'M TELLING YOU. THE BIRD WAS DEAD WHEN I GOT HERE."

Friday, January 11, afternoon

It is easy to get upset when you find out someone has lied to you. And there are also many ways to react to the lie. You can choose to politely point out the lie. Or just pretend to have fallen for it, which effectively means to deceive them back. Most times, I ignore and pretend indifference.

CHEAP LIFE IN AN OVER CONTROLLED CITY

Wednesday, January 16, afternoon

I live in a city and follow the kind of over controlled schedule only truly under-employed people can devise. I sleep till I wake and wake till I sleep. By mid-morning, I walk to a café that has become my office. In the evenings, I wander to the waterfront bridge to watch the setting sun or catch some pigeons by the downtown square. Can life get any cheaper and real?

MUDDY FEET IN THIS OVERCROWDED CITY

Tuesday, January 22, morning

Q: I wandered around the streets and decided to hit the bars last night. When I woke up this morning, my paws were bruised and covered with mud and dirt. I don't remember visiting a farm. Can anyone explain to me what happened?

A: Many wake up with the same problem after hitting the bars in this overcrowded city. Bars do get really crowded on a Monday evening so it's a given that a lot of people will step on your feet.

Define identity

Thursday, January 24, morning

I prefer an Internet connection to a car.
Facebook, Twitter, Instagram have become
my networking tools and newsrooms.
Offline, my dreams have become too
unreal and unattainable.

GROWING OLD IS MANDATORY.
GROWING UP IS OPTIONAL.

Wednesday, January 30, afternoon

At least that's what I've been told and hence, I am stuck in arrested development. I commit some of the alleged crimes of the adult generation these days.

1) Hide out in school
2) Travel to some far flung places in the name of peace keeping
3) Defer moving out
4) Being fickle in the job market

Flightiness may seem like the new yardstick. And there's absolutely nothing wrong with this.

Deceived

Friday, February 8, evening

So these are the dreams of adult
happiness

1) Rearing children
2) Paying off a mortgage loan
3) Working 60 hours a week
4) Getting squashed like cattle during
   morning peak hours

Be my valentine

Thursday, February 14, morning

It's alright if you are still looking for another single friend to tide through the day, because you are not the only one. You search through throng of friends on your social network, and those passing Polaroid-like snapshot relationships that have made it onto your Instagram pages. How technology has affected our love life in ways that would've been unimaginable 10 years ago.

Cat Samurai

Monday, February 18, afternoon

We've been raised to have an overly inflated emphasis on our own self-worth. So yeah, everyone loves a good job title. We've got ninjas to gurus as quirky back titles. But has anyone ever wonder what happens to our career path after a back title like ninja? To samurai? Not likely so.

HOW TO GET RICH

Friday, March 1, morning

Ever wonder why the rich only gets richer? Apparently, it's because they focus on earning the money. The middle class only focuses on saving the money. Stop saving and start spending?

STOP WORKING START THINKING

Thursday, March 7, morning

Middle class views starting a new business as a risky venture. That's why many tend to be salaried workers. The wealthy sees it as a road to wealth and economic freedom. They look for ideas that solve problems for other people and make money from those ideas. Stop working and start thinking?

STOP FEELING TO GET RICH

Wednesday, March 13, evening

Middle class sees money through the eyes of emotion. The wealthy see money through the eyes of logic. They don't fear losing, but instead they see money as a tool for greater options and opportunities. Start cold, hard logic and stop getting emotional?

STOP APOLOGISING

Monday, March 18, afternoon

Middle class has flexible deadlines and loosely defined goals. The wealthy have firm goals with "do or die" deadlines. Their goal is to make money and more money and they don't apologise for it. Stop apologising and start stepping toes?

Live below means

Wednesday, March 27, morning

Middle class live beyond their means. The wealthy live below their means. Rich people get richer quietly. They seldom spend money on jewellery or flashy things. The main desire for economic freedom is their main catalyst for success. They just want to be free instead of in debt. Stop spending and start saving? Err... refer to entry "How to get rich.", posted on Friday, March 1.

Humans

Wednesday, April 10, evening

Heartless and rude. They don't seem to understand the rights of property. Whenever I come across something good to eat, they take it away from me.

THIEVES AND AN OUTSIDER

Monday, April 15, morning

Thieves. That's why I have chosen to sleep instead of hunting for more. 14 hours of work haven't exactly paid off. I can no longer afford to pay for the things I want. Global economics have robbed me of my desires. I have technically just become an outsider.

Cat simple me

Friday, April 19, evening

I am a simple cat. What you see is what you get. When I feel tired, I sleep. When I am hungry, I eat. When I get angry, I bite and scratch. When I am sad, I utter my grief at a corner. There is nothing unpredictable about me. Why can't you be like me?

The Perfect Crime

Monday, April 22, afternoon

I stare unblinking at that piece of chocolate cake on Jane's desk. Of course it's not meant for me. Who am I kidding? But I have just been presented with a golden opportunity. This excellent window of space gives anyone an opportunity to do something even one normally would not do. Is this the perfect crime?

Complicated human me not

Monday, April 29, evening

I've always thought if I had gone to a barber and had my face shaven, I would look no different from a human. But I don't think I would ever want to be a human. There's nothing more complicated than human emotions and I am just a simple cat.

Lottery in My Dreams

Wednesday, May 8, morning

I have long been a collector of junk. Last night, I dreamt someone had picked up an old piece of junk I had discarded (obviously thinking it worthless). He studied it with interest and offered me a high price for it. When morning came and I woke up, it was obvious the piece of junk is still a worthless junk. Pitiful dream. I thought I had struck lottery.

"THE CAT FOLLOWS ME."

Wednesday, May 15, evening

"How was your day, darling?"
"Fine."
"Did you enjoy work?"
"Not really."
"Why not?"
"I don't know."
"Did anyone bully you?"
"I think my boss hates me."
"What makes you say that?"
"Just a feeling."
"What about your colleagues?"
"They hate my nose."
"They told you that?"
"No. I just think so. I hate my nose."
"Why?"
"It's too big."
"Don't be crazy."
"I'm not."
"You're saying crazy stuff."

"I'm not."
"Yes, you are."
"You're unbearable."
"You're nuts."
"We can't get along."
"No, we can't."
"Ok, let's call it quits then."
"Cool."
"The cat follows me."
"Fine."

Lonely in a Careful Way

Friday, May 31, evening

Quite often, I am lonely and alone. I see stuff most people probably don't notice, so it can be hard to find a genuine connection with anyone. What is really exciting to me often goes right over the heads of others. They tell me to find my flock, but I think loneliness would always stick to me. It's safe.

A BITTER MOMENT

Friday, June 14, morning

There is nothing as bitter as this moment when you step out of the house - still dark with only a tint of orange in the eastern sky. You are assaulted by the stagnant air, a hungry belly, and the prospect of a full day's work. You simply lose your tongue. There is no desire to speak to anyone.

Getting home first

Tuesday, June 18, evening

They forget to talk. They forget to think. Everyone in the evening jam is obsessed by one idea: to get home first.

Gassed Alive

Friday, June 21, afternoon

I inhale this bad air and my throat starts to burn. My eyes tear. My lungs on the brink of collapsing. I am being gassed alive by this ridiculous haze in the city. And I can do nothing about it.

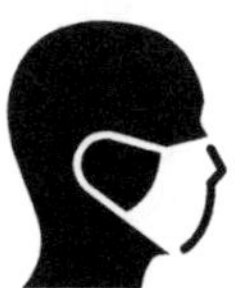

Persistent living

Tuesday, July 2, afternoon

It's through fantasies and dreams that we edit out the parts of our lives that make us uncomfortable. But fatigue sets in when you are stubbornly attached too long in a single dream. If only I know when to get out of one and buy into the next.

Twisted, not crooked

Friday, July 5, morning

Many people have asked me about my crooked tail. And they have too often judged and assumed being crooked may mean dishonest, evasive, and immoral since it is not straight. But crooked things may be as stiff and inflexible as straight; just as one may be as positive in error as in truth. Sounds twisted?

A MAJOR DISCONNECT

Wednesday, July 17, morning

I'm a pretty optimistic cat. And there are plenty of good news stories going around the world. But just looking at the numbers, it's clear that there is a major disconnect between sentiment and reality.

Judgement

Friday, July 19, evening

If there is one thing in the world that really upsets me, it is being known as the cat with a crooked tail. I can still remember the horror of discovering, maybe at the age of 2, when Vern started trying to straighten my tail, gave up and ended up writing a book about my crooked tail. Why? Why? Why? Why can't my tail be straighter, or curvier and just, not crooked?

Impassive

Thursday, July 25, morning

Once my bowl has been re-filled and re-stocked with tuna fish, I tend to lose interest in it. It simply becomes an object I neither like nor dislike. I suspect most parents feel this way about their grown up children.

ALTERATIONS

Wednesday, August 7, afternoon

Normally even the slightest hint of having to make alterations to my daily routine would have sent me into a state of frenzy. But I am given neither a choice nor a chance to protest in this matter. No matter, I still try to make it better.

OVERCOMING FEAR

Monday, August 12, morning

I used to be afraid of the darnedest things. Afraid of the flying cockroaches, the tiniest ants, the creepiest sounds. Now, I realise my fear of failing is becoming less than my fear of remaining unfulfilled. Hence, I'm stepping out today to count the number of steps to the front yard. There are a total of 21 steps.

MORTALITY IN SLOW MO

Wednesday, August 14, evening

There is no way to be alive without being conscious of the potential for disaster. One way or another, death hangs over all of us. Nobody is immune in this unstable and unpredictable world. It operates outside our ability to control it. That's why it's always good to take things slow. Smell the weeds.

Middling fears

Tuesday, September 3, evening

The return of fears: tapering fear, Syria fear, inflation fear, unemployment fear. The result of fears: stock market tanks, crumbling emerging market currencies, oil surges, gold jumps. Dare Devil said that a man with no fear is a man with no hope. I ought to be hopeful still...

YOU CAN'T BE THAT IMPORTANT.

Tuesday, September 10, morning

A: "How's work going?"
B: "I'm completely swamped. I haven't made it to the gym in weeks."
A: "Me, too. I feel like I'm living in the office."

You've clocked in 15 hours at work. Your shoulders are stiff and aching. You're having double visions. But let's face it. Are you seriously that important at work?

Passing relationships

Wednesday, September 25, evening

My life is full of passing relationships. People I knew for a nano-scroll on Google search (sometimes hours). Some who posed for Polaroid-like snapshots in my memory which outlast many of the long-exposure images I've collected since.

The Berlin Wall falls, the stock market crashes, presidents get shot, 2 government shut downs

Thursday, October 3, morning

We've all been through this 5 stages of grief: denial, anger, bargaining, depression, acceptance. We learn not to get too attached. We've seen marriages dissolve, the Berlin Wall falls, the stock market crashes, presidents get shot, 2 government shut downs, Michael Jackson and Whitney Houston die from drug overdose, and a very-out-to-shock-the-world Miley Cyrus. So let's just get back to our "meh meh meh". We shouldn't get too hurt, too shocked, too outraged. Just get zen.

Confessions of an Awkward Cat

Wednesday, October 4, evening

I tense up. I admit my mind is slow to accept changes. I still feel like the nervous, awkward cat and I wonder if I'm really capable of the vast amounts of responsibilities and increasing autonomy in front of me.

I won't lie. I'm scared shitless by this future. I feel like my dreams are still "out there," and I need more time to become better than what I am today.

I DID IT

Friday, October 25, morning

I thought I couldn't do it. But I surprised myself. There is a distinct difference between you thought you couldn't do it and selling yourself short by not believing you could do it.

I managed to creep onto the bed last night without Tom and Jane knowing it, and I slept, like a baby.

A VOYEUR AT 4A.M.

Monday, November 4, morning

At 4a.m., the city was asleep, and I was awake. The lack of social interactions never killed me, but it bothered me then. I would be lucky if I could find anyone coherent to talk to at this time. I became a voyeur while waiting for the break of dawn, and the smell of fresh newspapers.

I couldn't wait to do something useful.

A MURDERER AT 4P.M.

Monday, November 11, afternoon

At 4p.m., I lost all sense of time, and the ability to interact. Fatigue crashed into me after weeks of solitary confinement. With the sun on my back, I flipped through my mental day planner and ran down the list of to-dos.

It didn't make any sense at all. Didn't I just kill that damn rat an hour ago?

I SUCCUMB TO TEMPTATION. ONCE MORE.

Thursday, November 14, afternoon

I am not known for making extraordinary good decisions. I just do idiotic, impulsive, and risky things like making a kill for that piece of cake that's not meant for me. But the fact that it's been sitting there for the last 2 hours, untouched, uneaten, unguarded, I succumb to temptation. What a piece of heaven! It's great feeling like a teenager once more.

Monday starts Sunday

Sunday, November 17, morning

Did you already think two days for a weekend were too long not to get connected? You've started reading the Business Times, watching breaking news on CNBC, getting onto Twitter traffic on Sunday morning, and trying to decipher economics of the Monday market. Wouldn't it have been nicer to wake up late on a Sunday morning instead of getting back to work?

Suffocated in My Own Fur Coat

Tuesday, November 26, morning

I have a lot of possessions at home. A 14 inch box. Colour coordinated drapes. Statement furniture built for scratching. A wardrobe bursting with cheap fur. Boxes of processed food. Yet, with all these at home, I feel without one. I run. Suffocated in my own black fur. I guess home is when the fur comes off.

Millionaires This Festive Season

Monday, December 9, afternoon

I stand outside the mall in the cold, basking in the joys of this festive season. The mall's interior is decked out for Christmas: light-studded garlands, a gigantic 100 feet tall Christmas tree, and colossal rein deers. Everyone is uninterested by my presence. Their immediate attention have been grabbed by the endless amount of everything and anything in the mall. Money is plentiful and easy during this time of the year. People forget and spend like they are millionaires.

Anxiety

Monday, December 30, evening

I have always loved the aesthetics of Christmas holidays. But this year, I find myself utterly immune to all of it. As I walk down the strip, where all is bright and in abundance, I find myself feeling oddly side-stepped. I can't seem to care. Exhaustion and stress have made me difficult to talk, to interact. I experience a gripping anxiety about the cost of gas, food, movie tickets, and other necessary expenses in the coming year. And I get an overwhelming disassociation that makes everything difficult, and, at times, impossible.

About the Author

R.S. Vern is the creator of book trilogy series: Haee and the Other Middlings. The 1st part of this series won the International IndieReader Discovery Award in 2013.

An oddly conflicted soul, she finds herself constantly torn between the challenges of saving the world and the realities of making a living. She calls herself a middling - urbanised, uneased, and most of the time, in a flux.

Haee is a real cat living in her home. Instead of writing as herself, she feels that it is less brutal seeing life through the eyes of a cat.

R.S. Vern holds a B.A. in English Literature, an M.A. in Communications, and a G.D. in Applied Positive Psychology.

About Illustrated Series

For all ages. Illustrated book series "Haee and the Other Middlings" provides an insightful and delightful read at what it means to be functioning, breathing, and living as we are today.

Relatable and endearing, readers of all ages can find resonance in R.S. Vern's middling characters, both humans and cats. Far from perfect, the journey of its protagonist, cat Haee, serves as a reminder that the pursuit of meaning and purpose is an ongoing endeavour, and amidst our insecurities and imperfections, it is natural for our perspectives to shift and evolve.

Through the imaginative world of middlings, R.S. Vern creates a series of 3 beautifully illustrated novels that provokes thought and contemplation about what it means to live in this 21st century. At the end of it, Vern believes poignancy can also be hopeful as long as we continue our search, no matter.

Part I of this series wins the International IndieReader Discovery Award 2013.

www.ingramcontent.com/pod-product-compliance
Lightning Source LLC
LaVergne TN
LVHW010607160826
845677LV00013B/3299

* 9 7 8 9 8 1 1 8 6 8 6 2 7 *